The Lady Doth Protest
Famously Female

D. D. Holland

The Lady Doth Protest

D. D. Holland

Edited by Black Pear Press

First published in 2023 by Black Pear Press
http://www.blackpear.net
Copyright © D. D. Holland

ISBN 978-1-913418-89-2

Front cover image by Lisette-Elouise Wynn

Black Pear Press

Dedication

This book is dedicated to all the women who make me laugh and taught me to laugh through the pain—for Tina, Lorna, Charlotte, Sue, Pat and Emillie.

This book is also dedicated to all the people who think I'm funny (thanks, Mum).

With special thanks to Jack McGowan, Charley Barnes and Ruth Stacey, who taught me (amongst other things) not to take myself so seriously, and to the wonderful team at Black Pear.

With thanks to my Vo for testing the somnolence of my work with such unwavering dedication, and, I suppose, for his dogged love and support.

In loving memory of Nonna Jean and Granny Flower—I hope heaven is a hoot.

Contents

Famously Disobedient— The Fall of Eve

In the beginning, there was Adam, and he was hungry.

'It better not be bloody banana salad again,' he grumbled, picking his teeth with a sliver of bark.

'It isn't as though there's much else to choose from.' Eve glared at him and continued the peeling process. She took her time removing the stringy bits to avoid a repeat of yesterday's complaints. Adam pouted and scratched his fig leaf.

'I don't even like banana salad.'

Eve picked up the stirring stick from the least filthy rock.

'You could always cook your own dinner if you don't like the way I'm doing it.'

'You know I have an injury!' Adam said, rubbing his side. 'It hurts something terrible to reach up. I couldn't possibly move. In fact, I might never move again!'

He reclined further into his shaded bed, which he thought Eve really ought to make again before nightfall.

'Then maybe you should be grateful for what you're given,' Eve snapped, throwing the empty banana skins onto the pile. There was a tense silence, broken only by the sound of squelching banana. Adam continued to pick his teeth, glaring as Eve plated his portion of banana salad onto a banana-leaf. He snatched it from her and mashed it with his eating stick.

'Maybe *you* should try harder to bring variety to our diet,' he grumbled under his breath. Eve stirred her own meagre portion and ignored the gagging noises Adam made with each bite. There was a hiss as something wound itself around a low hanging vine, its vibrating tongue searching for the outline of Eve's ear.

'Maybe you should,' whispered the snake.

Famously Inanimate—
Getting Your Rocks Off

Pigmaleion was eloping. There was really no need. The town had long since taken to tactfully ignoring Pigmaleion and his eccentricities, but he was eloping anyway. He loaded his girlfriend, with great difficulty, onto a small fishing boat, and set sail for...anywhere else (he was an artist, not a navigationalist). Rocksy was many things, but being almost one entire tonne of solid marble, she wasn't dainty. The bottom of the boat ground the seabed as they struggled to meet open water. Pigmaleion covered her in a blanket. He didn't want filthy sailors destroying her virtue with their lecherous, prying eyes.

'There we are, my sweet. Wouldn't want you catching cold now, would we?'

Rocksy smiled at him, as she always did. Bobbing gently on the romantic Mediterranean Sea, Pigmaleion's thoughts turned to the idea of getting his Rocksy off.

'My love, you are more beautiful than a sky full of stars, than the golden sun! More beautiful than the Goddess of beauty herself, Aphrodi—'

'Ahem.'

Pigmaleion jumped, almost casting himself overboard. They were not alone in the boat.

'Your lordship! Your highness! Aphrodite, your majesty,' Pigmaleion stooped into a low bow.

The Goddess of Love sat on the edge of the boat, swinging her dark feet in the cool water. A gaggle of Erotes tittered beside her, their muscular bodies held aloft by the vociferous flapping of their tiny wings. They hummed soft, ethereal tunes as they twisted and dived, showering their mother with scented flower petals.

Alright, she was beautiful. I'm trying to tell you that kind of thing doesn't matter, but if you're the Goddess of Beauty, the dress code

2

calls for a little more than some high-heels and some tasteful make up. She wasn't beautiful like the meek and virginal paintings and statues men like to use to decorate museums; she was beautiful like a hurricane or a tsunami (viewed from a distance, of course). She was beautiful because her physical body was merely a vessel for the raw, unbridled beauty of natural power which flowed within the veins of every God. It is important to remember this when holding a conversation with her, if you don't want to be turned into an arachnid, or something even more unpleasant.

'Hello, Pigmaleion,' she said, lazily.

('She wants me,' Pigmaleion thought. 'Too bad I'm taken!')

'To what do I owe this mighty, auspicious honour, your most high and beautifulness?'

His nose brushed the salt speckled deck.

'Do get up, Pigmaleion. I've seen too many arse-kissers in my time without you adding to the number.'

Aphrodite pulled her curvaceous legs into the boat; one of the Erotes swooped down to dry her toes, and another dried the end of her braids, so long they grazed the surface of the sea.

'I heard on the breeze that you have fallen fervently in love with a statue, am I correct?'

'Yes, this is she—I call her Rocksy!' Pigmaleion pointed to his wife, who held out her hand, as she always did, to Aphrodite. Aphrodite was tempted to take it. She examined the cold, pale face.

'Well, well, she is a very pretty thing indeed. Perhaps a little meek-looking, a little insipidly docile, but certainly very fine. You have outdone yourself with such craftsmanship.'

'Thank you, my lady. I, of course, based her on likenesses of you…'

'Of course,' Aphrodite said, the corners of her mouth twitching. It was good to know that rumours of her awesome power had seeped even into the tales of the islanders. Alongside beauty, one must command respect and fear, otherwise the whole thing is a complete waste.

Aphrodite twitched the blanket aside to better admire the statue's perfect form.

'You really love her, Pigmaleion? You, who I have heard from the townsfolk, are a horrid hater of women?'

Pigmaleion had no idea where she had heard such vicious lies and threw himself into Rocksy's protective embrace.

'Oh yes, ma'am. She never answers back, she's always up for it, she never ages a day—she's perfect!'

'I see.'

Pigmaleion hesitated.

'She is also more beautiful than the waves of the ever-flowing ocean, purer than the light of the whitest star, more perfect than the veins which weave patterns into the skeletons of autumn leaves—'

Aphrodite smiled. This was the kind of adoration she recognised.

'Such pure love brings joy to my heart, especially from a man thought only capable of hate. I will give you a gift.'

'A gift, Majesty? I've done nothing to deserve a gift.'

Aphrodite smiled. Two fruit-flies that had been circling opposite ends of the boat met above her head and immediately flew off to find some privacy.

'No, but you shall have one, nonetheless. So you might experience true marital bliss with your wife of stone, I shall grant her life.'

'Life!' Pigmaleion gasped, throwing himself at her feet. 'Oh, great goddess, you are truly the most beauteous, most benevolent, most bountiful of all the gods on Olympus!'

'Yes,' Aphrodite agreed, 'although I wouldn't say that too loudly. Zeus could be round here looking for his latest girlfriend. We already had a swan, the next could be another seemingly obscure form of waterfowl.'

'Oh majesty, Rocksy's only flaw is she cannot say that she loves me too! A thousand thanks, a million thanks—'

4

Aphrodite, who had other places to be that evening, crossed the boat in several graceful steps and pulled down one side of the blanket, revealing a single pert marble breast. A wind rose, the boat rocked and groaned. The Erotes, who had been beneath the water causing complications in the relationships of the surrounding fish, huddled together at the opposite end of the boat, their wings protecting their nakedness from the whipping sea foam.

Aphrodite raised a delicate hand and placed it upon Rocksy's breast. After several minutes of apparently fruitless silence, bar the lapping of the waves against the side of the boat, Pigmaleion thought he heard it. The thud. The single, heavy, mechanical thud of an unsure heart. The breast quivered beneath Aphrodite's fingers. The beat was followed by another beat, and another, a pale blue spider's web blooming from her chest, veins dancing and gyrating as they wove delicate patterns beneath her skin. Where the veins wove, colour followed, white skin blooming into a healthy, delicate pink; fingers twitching as life sprang into Rocksy's very fingernails. Soon, she stood, naked as the day she was carved, on her podium, shivering as the salt spray hit her newly be-fleshed body.

Pigmaleion's mouth dropped open. Aphrodite removed her hand from Rocksy's breast before things got awkward.

'For Olympus' sake, don't just stand there! There's no point breathing life into a woman if you're just going to watch her freeze to death!'

'Oh, yes! Of course...' Pigmaleion handed Rocksy the blanket which had fallen from her shoulders, blushing. She took it with a hand still unsure as to the finer details of muscular contraction.

'You're pleased?'

Pigmaleion nodded enthusiastically.

'Oh yes, she's perfect! Not tainted or defiled like normal women— every inch of her, man-made!' Pigmaleion circled his lover. She shivered as her new brain attempted to fathom the meaning of the cold which stung her cheeks and the warmth of the woollen blanket which made her hairless armpits sweat. As he circled, Pigmaleion wished he had carved her left ankle a little thinner…perhaps added an inch to her buttocks and removed one from her neck…

'She's a great beauty,' Aphrodite agreed. 'You must look after her well. She's new to this world and will need much instruction as to its splendours and…failings.'

'Yes, quite,' Pigmaleion muttered. 'And to think, I was going to settle for a princess! She's no mere princess. She's the daughter of a goddess!'

'Er, yes. And with that thought fresh in our heads, I'll leave you and my daughter alone to whatever it is you do together,' Aphrodite said, offering her hands to her attending Erotes.

'Oh, and Pigmaleion?'

'Mmm?'

'I've changed her name. You know how it is, something a little more dramatic for the headlines…a little less, on the nose?'

'Oh, yes. Not a problem, thank you, your highness!'

But Aphrodite had already stepped off the boat and melted into the sea breeze.

Pigmaleion turned to his animated bride. He had struggled to control his excitement in the presence of Aphrodite, but now she was gone. He wasted no time in ripping off his toga, revealing his wrinkled, naked form.

'My beautiful wife! Come into my arms!'

Pigmaleion's girlfriend stepped delicately down from her podium, her warm arms reaching out for her lover.

'Hello,' she beamed, exposing her shining set of perfect teeth. 'My name's Galatea.'

Pigmaleion wrinkled his nose. She had an Athenian accent. A gruff, unbecoming Athenian accent. And her teeth were too big. And she wasn't as pretty when she was moving as she was when she had been still. And Galatea was a stupid name, nowhere near as sexy as Rocksy.

'Bollocks,' Pigmaleion muttered, flipping the oars and turning the boat back around. 'I've gone right off her.'

Famously Servile—
The Mother, The Whore and The Crone

'Well, I think it's a damn shame,' Mary said to Mary, whilst Mary sobbed without stopping for breath.

'Aye. Tis that,' Mary replied, patting Mary awkwardly on the shoulder.

Mary nodded through her tears and blew her nose violently into the handkerchief offered to her.

'I don't like it at all. He says, "Peace and Love" and this is where it gets him.' Mary sniffed and drew her shawl tighter around her shoulders.

'He says, "Peace and Love" an' they says "Nail 'im up",' Mary agreed, shaking her head. 'He wasn't no harm to nobody. Just 'ad 'is own little cult who went around givin' blankets to the homeless and bashin' the odd noble lord or thievin' tax collector over the 'ead when they deserved it. Tain't punishable by death, surely? The whole world's gone mad.'

Mary's weeping intensified to wailing. The other two Marys instinctively placed a hand on each shoulder.

'And I'll tell you what really steams my terrine—' (Mary scowled, her terrine well and truly steamed) '—where are the rest of them? I'll tell you where; they're all at home writing up their memoirs!'

'They never?' Mary gasped.

'They are! They think they can make a buck. When he was alive, he would never have let them cash in on it. He didn't believe in taking money from the poor. He would tell them what he thought for free!' Mary wrung the ends of her shawl in suppressed anger.

'I don't believe it! Who's at it then?' Mary leant in, hoping to receive the gossip via osmosis.

'Oh, they're all at it now! I think Matthew started it, but who knows?'

'Unnatural, it is,' Mary interjected. 'Sittin' there writin' in the dark all day about who he favoured most and what he meant by things. Usually, he meant what he said. Very straight-talkin'-like he was.'

'He was indeed,' Mary agreed.

'Called a jug a "jug", an idiot an "idiot" and a fish "lunch" he did,' Mary finished.

'I heard him say it! At that supper we had, (thinking about it, it was probably the last one), he said VERY EXPLICITLY that they weren't to make money out of this.'

'I 'eard 'im say that on multiple occasions,' Mary confirmed.

The Marys broke off the conversation to watch another cross being hauled up on the next hill over. All three shook their heads. Mary, who had just stopped crying, started up again with vigour. During this lull in the conversation, Mary had been considering the memoirs.

'I wonder how they'll differentiate between all the Marys?' Mary pondered.

'Ay, now, you don't think they'll write about us, do you?'

'I should think so! We bloody well did our fair share. Just because we're women and no one will teach us to read or write doesn't mean we aren't part of the story.'

Mary furrowed her brow.

'You're right. We've 'ad plenty to say over the years. He wouldn't have 'ad half as many followers if I 'adn't washed that loincloth of his regular. They better say somethin' nice. Who do they think cooked that last supper?'

'Exactly, Mary,' Mary said, considering how out of pocket she was since she'd been introduced to the concept of charity.

Riled by the thought that her cookery might not be canonised, (as a particularly splendid lamb terrine always should be), Mary looked over at the other Marys and realised that though there were many Marys, there was only one *Mary*. The others were nice girls, but they couldn't turn a flatbread like she could. They hadn't tried to raise a child who only spoke in proverbs, and they had absolutely not had to wash a well-worn loin cloth. This matter suddenly became one of great importance to her.

'How are they goin' to tell us apart? There'll be a lot of Marys to consider. Mary that Mark's mam, Mary that-James-and-Joseph's mam, Mary what-calls-herself Salome, Mary what-has-a-reputation-an'-comes-from-Bethany...' Mary scratched under her mourning veil. 'Mayhaps I'll be the "Wise Mary"? or the "Not-afraid-to-give-the-saviour-a-good-clip-around-the-ear-hole Mary"?'

Mary stopped her sniffling long enough to interject.

'Perhaps I will be the "Loyal Mary"?'

'Or "Wet Mary"...' Mary muttered to Mary, who stifled a laugh.

'I like to think they'll say something nice about me,' Mary pondered. 'Perhaps, "Kind Mary", or "Funded-most-of-the-bloody-trip Mary" or "What-a-nice-pair-of-melons Mary".'

Mary winked exaggeratedly to the Marys. Mary even raised a smile.

'Ooh, Mary!' Mary exclaimed with a chuckle, 'Talk like that an' they'll call you "Prostitute Mary"!'

Famously Kidnapped—
Greek Pride

'Walk me through this again—' (Helen's voice said, muffled through the sack) '—you had to judge who was the sexiest out of Hera, Athena and Aphrodite?'

'Uh-huh,' Paris grunted. Helen may be the most beautiful woman in the world, but she certainly wasn't the lightest.

'And Zeus chose you to judge because you were renowned for being fair?'

'Uh-huh. Ares bull.'

'Right. Then all three of them tried to bribe you…'

'Yup.' Paris panted asthmatically.

'…and, for personal reasons, you insisted it was impossible to judge whilst they were clothed, so had them strip?'

'In the interests of a fair trial, yes.'

'Uh-huh, and although Hera was the most beautiful, you chose Aphrodite because she's the best showman, and also bribed you the best,' Helen concluded.

'That's about the long and short of it. It was awfully close. All came down to the width of the nipples.'

'So, an impartial judge, allowed themselves to be bribed?'
Paris sighed.

'I've already told you, it's not biased judging if everyone bribes you.'

'That's the bit I'm getting stuck on,' Helen murmured.

'I won you, fair and square.' Paris offered a tentative pat on the rump, received with a sharp elbow to the spine.

'I don't think you did. At least Menelaus fought and won me. You just came and plucked me from my bed.'

Paris, known for liking women and absolutely not liking fighting, glanced nervously over his shoulder.

'Are we going to run all the way to Troy?' she finally asked. 'Because

I get travel sick.'

She retched and as Paris was wearing a new chiton that he didn't fancy washing, he was glad they had reached the water's edge.

'No.' He dropped her indelicately on the sand and pulled the sack from her head. 'Now get in the boat.'

'No.' Helen, capable of such stubbornness that continents were comparatively flexible, made herself comfortable on the ground.

Paris stared at her, discovering that the most beautiful women in the world tend to be the most disobedient. He stooped to lift her, and rather than fighting him, she laid down and became a dead weight. With much asthmatic wheezing, Paris rolled Helen, dishevelled and covered in sand, onto the boat.

They cast off, bobbing towards the ship waiting offshore. Clouds of dust erupted from the distant hillside.

'Now you're in trouble.'

Helen launched herself from the boat. Paris, used to women attempting to escape his affections, anchored down the end of her peplos. After a brief sea battle, resulting in one party having to dangle his little trojan soldier in a bucket of cool seawater, Helen was finally on the ship travelling away from Sparta. She watched dismally as Menelaus and his troops assembled on the beach.

'HELEN!' Menelaus shouted.

'MENELAUS!'

'I'LL COME AND FIND YOU!' Menelaus walked his horse into the sea to keep up with the ship.

'GOOD! DON'T FORGET TO CASH IN THAT TYNDAREUS OATH THING. THE PAPERWORK IS TO THE LEFT OF THE GRINDSTONE ON THE THIRD SHELF ABOVE THE PAINTED PLATE FROM YOUR MOTHER,' Helen bellowed.

'HELEN…. GRINDSTONE…. MOTHER'S PLATE AWAY TO A RAFFLE…ON MY WAY!' Were the only words Helen caught of Menelaus' parting speech.

She sat down hard on a bundle of fishing nets.

Paris glowered at her from his water-bath. Helen glowered back.

'Don't you have a wife?' she accused.

'And a son. But I'm a wild stallion. Oenone understands this body is a gift to be shared with the world.'

Helen peered into the bucket and drew her own conclusions as to what Oenone's opinion was.

'I'm actually a lesbian,' said Helen, casually. 'Not that anyone cares. See a pretty woman and every man in Greece thinks he's entitled to her. I've been carrying on with Hero, my sexy Histrian handmaid, for years.'

Paris almost kicked over his bucket.

'You're lying!' He scrutinised her face, but it remained as stubborn as that of a particularly large ox stood in the middle of a particularly busy road, during a particularly hectic rush hour.

'That's not fair!' He wailed. 'You can't be a lesbian. You've got a daughter. You're trying to trick me!'

'Hermione? Oh, she's adopted. You didn't think the most beautiful woman in the world could adhere to male beauty standards post-partum, did you?'

Paris shook his head.

'You're too beautiful to be a lesbian.'

Helen narrowed her eyes and fixed an escaping curl.

'That displays a fundamental misunderstanding of homosexuality,' she sniffed. 'Just because I'm beautiful doesn't mean I should be passed around hordes of horny Greek men. I'm not a sex toy with a wig on.'

For a moment it looked as though Paris was rethinking his plan, but thinking did not come naturally to Paris.

'I'll take you to Troy anyway. Eventually my good looks and charm will enchant the gay right out of you!'

Helen did not roll her eyes.

'Enchant the gay out of me?'

Paris nodded.

'Then you can experience my excellent loving first hand, and as the most beautiful people in the world, we will have the world's most beautiful babies!'

This time, Helen did roll her eyes.

'Look, I don't have much choice, so I'll come to Troy with you. But I'm warning you now, I don't think it'll end well.'

Famously Burnt— St Joan of the Tin Hat

She arrived in a puff of smoke. Well, more like a cloud of smoke, billowing nebulously around her limbs. Her eyebrows were singed, her armour charred, but her spirit very much intact.

Gabriel stood behind the golden lectern and raised his arms. A choir of angels belted out a complicated tune. Above the din, Gabriel spoke.

'Welcome, Joan of Arc, humble servant of the Lord our God. You have lived a life of simplicity and piety, so enter now, this, the Kingdom of Heaven.'

The angels were really going for it by now. The din of three hundred middle-aged men all singing falsetto must be heard to be believed. They clung desperately to the last (and most painful) note, waiting for Joan to step through the gates.

She stood, arms folded across her chest, still smoking slightly, waiting for the angels to run out of breath.

After several minutes and several resuscitations, silence fell.

'I'm not going in.'

'What?'

'I'm not going in. I'm 19 years old. I did everything you told me, and I've been burnt to a crisp. It's not fair and I'm not going in. Send me back.'

'Er, we don't really do resurrections any more…' Gabriel scratched his halo and shooed the remaining members of the choir away.

Joan narrowed her eyes as though imagining a large target forming on Gabriel's forehead.

'Er, shall I get the big man?' he said, trying to dodge her intense gaze.

'That would probably be a good idea.'

Gabriel shot off through the pearly gates. Joan took the time to

15

sharpen her sword. When he reappeared, he wasn't alone. God threw up his arms, and the gates flew open.

'Joan! Good to see you again, what a marvellous job you did—'

Joan's sword swung uncomfortably close to the top of God's whiskers.

'You said it wouldn't happen again.'

God leant out of striking range and sidled behind Gabriel's lectern. He risked a side glance at Gabriel, who avoided his eye.

'Er, I didn't think it would, especially since you're a girl. I thought they would go easy on you.'

'Easy on me! The bible says women will cause Armageddon!'

'I don't think it says that exactly…'

'Eccles. 25.22, "of the woman came the beginning of sin, and through her, we all die".'

God raised an eyebrow at Gabriel, who nodded.

'Ah, I think I may have been misquoted…'

'And you can stone women to death for adultery.'

'Er..'

'Deuteronomy 22:24.'

'That does seem a little melodramatic…'

Joan raised her eyebrows, her armour clinking as she folded her arms.

Gabriel edged towards the pearly gates, but God caught the tip of a wing without taking his eyes off Joan.

'We take your complaints very seriously here. Allow me a few moments to discuss the situation with my colleague.'

God dragged Gabriel behind the lectern and ducked.

'What does it say all that "stone women" stuff for? I thought I told you to send a message of peace and love?' God hissed.

'It's not my fault! I told you, making people hear voices rather than sending someone in person was a bad idea! You can't always find a good signal and they get things wrong. "Celibate" and "celebrate" sound awfully similar if the connection is bad.'

'She seemed to hear everything all right!'

'She wore a tin hat most of the time, so it was easier to get through! It's a very good conductor.'

'Is there a verse about wearing tin hats?' said God.

'Not that I'm aware of, boss.'

'Can we put one in?'

'Probably not the best idea. They'll only write something about sinning cats instead, and next thing you know, we'll have a line of charred, disgruntled moggies queuing up at the gate.'

God sighed and kneaded his forehead.

'I don't know, drowning babies last week, stoning the women this week. Are there any other...discrepancies I should be aware of?' he said, gripping Gabriel's wing a little tighter.

'No,' Gabriel squeaked, determined not to be on shift when God found out about the passage on genocide, a miscommunication on a monumental scale which was colloquially referred to as "No one was spared, not even the donkeys". (1 Samuel 15:3: Now go and smite Amalek, and utterly destroy all that they have, and spare them not; but slay both man and woman, infant and suckling, ox and sheep, camel and ass).

'What about her?'

Gabriel shrugged.

'Not a lot you can do, boss.'

'I could try a resurrection?' God offered.

Joan rested her elbows upon the lectern and her chin upon her hand, looking down upon the two caretakers of heaven.

'They did burn me three times.'

'Hm. That is quite dead,' God grumbled. He sat on the edge of a cloud, his head in his wizened hands.

'I don't know, maybe I should give up on the whole prophet thing? It hasn't ended well for anyone. Crucifixions, upside-down

17

crucifixions, skinned alive, burned alive, drowned. Maybe we should send animals instead?'

Gabriel and Joan exchanged a glance.

'I'm don't think talking animals will go down so well, boss. We had the snake, we tried Balaam's donkey, but er...' (Gabriel loosened the collar of his smock and shot Joan a pleading look) 'for some reason people still aren't treating the donkeys right.'

'Aren't they?' God looked up, visibly distressed.

'No, boss, it's very strange.'

Joan pursed her lips.

God sighed.

'Surely they're nearly done with all these religious killings,' he said. 'It must be running out of steam. There are only so many people you can kill in the name of me.'

Gabriel risked a look over the clouds.

'I'm sure it's fine,' he thought. 'Inquisitions just ask people questions. Can't see the harm in that.'

Famously Ugly—
Weird Cousins

'When shall we three meet again, in thunder, lightning or in rain?' said the first.

'We could wait until the weather picks up a bit. The spells don't work as well if you get the parchment wet,' said the second.

'Shut up, you two, it's bloody awful out there and I'm not coming back out again,' said the third.

'I don't see why we should find him, anyway. Give me one good reason why he can't come and find us his-bloody-self. He's got legs, hain't he?' the second continued.

'I dunno. That's the issue with battle, isn't it? If he had some this morning, he might not by lunch. I suppose that's why the prophecy isn't specific. How much longer do we have to stand in this rain, Morag?'

'Shut up, Bridget, here he comes.'

'How do you know that's him?' Seonag interjected.

'He's the only one smiling when he kills people. Don't you have eyes?'

'Ah.'

'Oi! You! Cooee, yes, I'm talking to you. Come 'ere a minute!'

Macbeth had the physique of a tall man who had shrunk in the wash. His appearance implied a density, which upon initiating conversation became increasingly apparent. He lumbered over to the three women, forgetting to let go of the limb he had just severed from an unfortunate enemy. He peered at the women through the drizzle.

'Speak, if you can. What are you?' Macbeth's pupils dilated in a way which implied that he didn't have to tell you he was going to kill you because he was going to show you first.

'What does he mean "what are we"?' said Seonag.

'Cheeky so and so, clearly we're women!' Bridget rearranged her corsets.

'You're not…witches, are you?' Macbeth whispered.

Bridget bristled.

'We prefer occultly-gifted females if it's all the same to you.'

'Speak, crone!' Macbeth brandished his recently acquired third leg in her direction.

'Crone? This bloke is pushing his luck, Morag!' Seonag the occultly-gifted female, said.

Macbeth took a holiday from this conversation to assist a passing warrior in removing his helmet by an effective but messy method.

'Have you got a prophecy for me or what?' he said, returning to the women.

'Prophecy's a strong word. It's more like an…observation,' Morag said.

'Tell me my prophecy, crone!'

'Ooh, call me crone one more time, laddie!'

'Go on, witch!' People rarely had the chance to observe that Macbeth's people skills were lacking. Posthumously, though, the complaints were racking up against him.

Morag gripped Bridget's arm to silence her.

'There aren't many people standing between you and being king.'

'Go on?' Macbeth leant in.

'That's it. If you make important friends and good choices, you could be king one day,' said Morag.

'So you're saying I should kill everyone and become king?'

'Er, no,' said Saonag. 'You said that. We said to be nice to everybody and work your way up.'

'But murder is morally wrong?'

'We know,' said Bridget. 'Which is why we strongly advise against it.'

'Really,' said Morag. 'Don't murder anybody, that would be a bad idea.'

'Very bad,' agreed Seonag.

'Thank you, crones! I will fulfil my destiny!' Macbeth was already running away over the muddy field, sword in hand. He brandished his third leg at passing enemies, which was enough to shock anyone into surrender.

'Oi! Wait!' Bridget called. 'You won't kill anyone, will you?'

But he had disappeared into the blur of steel and screams. She turned to Morag.

'That didn't go as planned, did it?'

'Not really. I rather think he got the wrong end of the stick.'

Famously Ambitious— Lady Macbeth

'Out, damned Spot!' Lady Macbeth cried, scrubbing the shirt harder across the washboard. She threw it down into the basin rather childishly and collapsed into a chair.

' "Marry a rich man," you said. "You'll never have to do a day's work in your life," you said,' she muttered under her breath.

'Don't blame me!' Grandmama Macbeth retorted, her toothless mouth full of porridge. 'I ne'er told you to pick one that was off his rocker!'

'I didn't know that at the time, did I? He didn't engrave it under his portrait; "Noble Scottish lord in possession of a good fortune and a large bagpipe also happens to be a psychotic mass murderer, time wasters need not apply",' Lady Macbeth moaned, picking at the flaking skin on her hands.

'Aww, Betty, it isn't all bad. We have this nice castle, and if he carries on, he might even become king! You'd like that, Betty, you would. Queenhood would suit you.'

'What's the good of being a Queen with no servants, Mama? He's either killed them or they've left before he can. No good being the Queen if you have to wash your own bloody knickers.'

'Aw, pet,' Grandmama Macbeth put down her ear trumpet and continued to make sympathetic faces. That usually did the trick.

'Do you know he's telling everyone that I make him murder people? The cheek of it. The noblemen whine that I took a fine man and made him doolally. No one ever considered that I took a doolally man and am now stuck with a doolally man. Politics isn't fair, Mama, if they weren't complaining that I supported his sprees, they would complain that I didn't! Aren't I supposed to be obedient to my husband?' Lady Macbeth would have quite happily had the same conversation every night, but she was cut short.

Somewhere in the recesses of the rickety old castle, a door slammed.

'Here he comes, back to blight us with a bit more insanity.'

'Eh?' Grandmama Macbeth was fishing oats out of her dentures.

Macbeth appeared in the doorway, dragging a suspiciously weighted sack behind him.

'Evening dear,' Lady Macbeth ventured.

Macbeth turned slowly to look at his wife, his eyes wide and heavily dilated.

'Evening, oh vicious and murderous one,' he whispered.

'No, darling, that's you. You're the vicious murderer, remember?'

Macbeth's right eye twitched.

'Your hands, they're bleeding!' he cried. Lady Macbeth's enduring shred of patience was frazzling.

'Yes, you fool, trying to get the blood out of your shirts has got me in quite a vicious cycle. I keep telling you, if you're going to go out on a murdering spree, could you please put your shirts down for washing immediately after? You wait for the blood to congeal and then I can never get it out.' Lady Macbeth turned her back on her husband to stare determinedly out of the window.

'There you said it! The murdering spree! You force my hand, you witch, you hag! I was a good man, I never killed or maimed, then I married you and suddenly…murder!'

'Not this again, I've told you before. You can go on your murder sprees, just leave me out of it! If I wanted someone dead, I would do it myself. At least I would generate less laundry.'

Macbeth was not listening. He was staring at his hands and talking to ghosts.

'She made me do it! She's driven me mad!' He wailed and disappeared down the corridor, the echoes of his torment continuing to reverberate off the walls. Lady Macbeth shut the door. Sometimes when he started wailing, he could go on for hours.

'I wouldn't worry about it, Betty,' Grandmama interjected. 'All men have their little quirks. Your dad had a thing for fishing and if you think you have a problem, just wait until you're trying to scrub the smell of haddock off someone's codpiece.'

Lady Macbeth wasn't listening. She was staring out of the window again, feeling sorry for herself.

'I always get the blame for everything,' she lamented.

Famously Naked—
The Bare-Back Rider

'You've proved your point.' Leofric tugged at her arm.

'Not yet, I don't think. Besides, I've promised the people now, it wouldn't be fair to disappoint.' Lady Godiva smiled at her husband.

'Get off the horse,' he hissed, tugging a little harder.

'No,' she replied, jovial but firm. Well, not as firm as she used to be, she had already been widowed once and, though ageing gracefully, was ageing none the less.

'Come on, Tom!' she called. The lithe blacksmith trotted forward until their horses were parallel.

'Who's he?' Leofric choked. Despite strict orders not to look upon pain of death, he could feel the eyes of the housecarls beating down upon his wife's voluptuous body.

'He's going to be my bodyguard.'

'He's bloody well not!'

The glare from Tom's oiled muscles made Leofric's eyes water.

'Yes, he is, or I might be attacked in the street. You know what those peasants are like. They'll be trying to sell bits of me to pilgrims before I've had a chance to dismount.' The Lady patted Tom's knee.

Leofric blustered, flustered, and deflated.

'Fine. Tom can go, but only if he puts his kit back on. I see no reason he should be naked, too.'

'Oh. That was just personal preference,' she winked.

Eventually, they were ready to ride out of the castle gates.

'For the last time, Goddy, you've proved your point, I'll lower the tax. Get off the horse and come inside.'

Lady Godiva waved her husband away.

'No going back now, Leo! I'll see you later. Keep an eye on the children!'

Nine sets of fascinated eyes watched their mother ride out of the gate from an arrow slit above the north tower, disturbed because not only was their mother naked, but their father was in charge of arranging breakfast.

'Be home before dark!' Leofric called after his wife in his most authoritative voice.

'And no peeping, Tom!'

Neither responded. Leofric stared at the castle's apparently abandoned windows before pulling his hat down over his eyes and retreating inside. As he opened the front door, he was sucked into the castle by a vacuum caused by the sheer speed of three hundred bodies disappearing at once. He moved his office into the wine cellar for the day.

*

'I feel very safe with you, Tom.' Lady Godiva remarked as they followed the road at an amble (to reduce chafing).

'So you should, my lady. I'm prepared to put my body between you and almost anything. The ground, a bed, even a horse, if you're feeling inventive.'

Lady Godiva laughed, and Tom remained hopeful.

As they rode into town, the shutters and doors were shut tight. If one were to look carefully, however, one would notice that in every house, at least one shutter had been mysteriously shaved down just enough to form a peephole large enough for a family to peer through if they stacked themselves the right way. Lady Godiva waved enthusiastically, though of course, she couldn't see how many people waved back.

'Enjoying yourself, my lady?' Tom raised a brow.

'I am rather. I've always found clothes a bit, well, restrictive. Not to mention unhygienic. How many creepy crawlies do you think live in the fabric of a medieval lady's dress, Tom?'

Tom shrugged.

'Well, I can tell you it's a lot. I've actually been wearing fewer clothes around the house recently, and it may be too much information, but the pox marks on my bottom have eased tremendously. You should try it.'

Tom shook his head.

'Naked smithing is probably not a good idea. You couldn't get close enough to the fire. Thinking about it, you wouldn't want to get too close to the anvil either. Nah, I think I had better stick to wearing clothes, at least for work.'

'Perhaps nudity isn't for everyone,' Lady Godiva nodded gravely.

They rode in silence for a few more yards, with only the thuds of old men hitting the floor and the squawks of domestic tiffs regarding the proximity of one's spouse to that of the first prototype of the binocular, to break the silence. (A device man apparently did not find need for again until 1825, when history cannot tell us exactly *which* lady appeared *sans vêtements*, but we can assume one probably was).

They neared the end of the high street just as the morning sun was making the ride a slightly less bracing experience.

Lady Godiva's horse stooped to drink from a trough outside the inn. An eager minstrel twanged behind the shutters. He was quickly learning that the English language was unforgivably lacking in words which rhymed with 'nipple'.

'You know, I think this is a stand for all women,' The Lady said, shaking out her greying hair to the sound of a lyre-string snapping. 'Here I am, in my sunset years, having carried and birthed nine children, not afraid to get my kit off for a good cause. I really hope they make some good paintings of me, you know, to inspire other women. Stretch marks, stretched tummy, wrinkles and all.'

'I shouldn't worry, my lady. I should think there's an explicit woodblock already in circulation,' Tom said, with the innocence of a man who had not already commissioned an explicit woodblock to be stamped into the latest edition of 'Blacksmiths and Babes—Caution, Blistering Hot!'. 'They'll be talking about this for many years to come.'

Lady Godiva blushed in a pleased sort of way.

'Ah tush, they'll never remember this. Those enormous donations I've made to the church are much more memorable than the fact I liked to walk around with my boobs out,' she said.

Famously Beheaded—
The Witch-Queen

Anne stared out the window with a determination which would have cut glass had the windows of her cell possessed any.

The door swung open.

'It's time to go, miss.' The gaoler, William Kingston, refused to enter the room. He'd heard rumours about witches and didn't fancy spending the rest of his life catching flies and saying 'Ribbit'.

'I'm not going,' Anne said, continuing to stare at a blade of grass three storeys below.

'Don't be like that. It'll be a fair trial.'

'Fair trial!' Anne repeated. 'I'm fighting for my life, accused of sleeping with half of London and my own brother because my husband's leaving me for the help. Alright, I haven't produced him a son, but two wives in and he's only had girls, himself being the common factor...I'll be tried by a jury consisting of my bitter ex-fiancé, an uncle who can't vote in my favour otherwise he'll be accused of sleeping with me too, and the man who wants me dead. If you could underline which bits of this trial you consider "fair", I'm sure I would appreciate it.'

Kingston's mouth hung open, catching flies. He gestured hopefully to the door. Anne sighed and brushed off her skirts.

'Fine, let's see who I've been sleeping with today. They haven't called any donkeys as witnesses, have they? No sheep stood in the box? "The queen was heard to remark that this was a particularly beautiful horse, then spent the rest of the afternoon riding it...." '

Anne didn't stop talking until they reached the courtroom. The door swung open to reveal a man wearing a smirk so unattractive that—like the sun—it was impossible to look at directly.

Thomas Cromwell was a large and vicious-looking rat, as though he had got this large by eating all the other rats (which, in a metaphorical sense, he had). The most disarming thing about Cromwell was his voice. He spoke with no intonation or punctuation at all. This made it difficult to distinguish between questions, answers, and statements and had led to problems throughout Cromwell's career. As it turns out, the phrase 'I have time to kill someone send in a prisoner' urgently needs punctuating.

Anne stomped noisily from the door to her seat, and then searched her many layers of rustling petticoats for a handkerchief, 'Just in case Cromwell said something nice'.

'Where's my defence, then?' Anne made deliberate eye contact with several of her previous friends.

'A defence won't be necessary.' Cromwell's excitement set his long nose aquiver in a particularly rodential manner.

'Kingston will be my defence lawyer then.'

The court exchanged glances.

'Absolutely not, you are not Queen in this court,' Cromwell said, a smile spreading over his face like a bloodstain.

'Fine. Then I shan't plead anything. I'll just sit here.' Anne illustrated this by staring blankly at her fingernails. Muttering erupted. Without a plea, the entire process would be stalled.

Cromwell's cheeks blistered red.

'You're making a mockery of this whole thing!' he hissed.

'I haven't had to try very hard.'

'Fine,' Cromwell blustered.

Anne patted the seat beside her and looked expectantly at Kingston.

Kingston shot a terrified glance at Cromwell—who indicated he should get on with it—and sat next to Anne.

Anne smiled.

'Not guilty,' she said.

'We aren't at that bit yet,' he hissed.

She shrugged.

Cromwell eyed Anne like a butcher deciding the quality of a steak. It was a fact widely known but little discussed that Cromwell had always fancied Anne and was most put out when she married the king.

'The Duke of Norfolk will read the charges.'

Anne yawned as the list of adulterous charges rambled on. She poked Kingston in the side.

'How many acts of carnal pleasure are we up to now?'

'Er…twenty.'

'Twenty!' Anne scoffed. 'Barely covers a weekend!' She winked. Kingston blushed and avoided her eye.

The list finally at an end, Anne raised her hand.

Cromwell ignored it.

She raised the other.

He continued with proceedings.

She stood up and waved.

He spoke louder.

'Anne Boleyn, is there anything you have to say in your defence?'

Anne jumped.

'Oh yes. Cromwell. I have alibis for twelve of the occasions I was supposedly astride one or the other of these men.'

'Aha, but as a witch, you simply duplicated yourself so you could simultaneously sodomise Francis Weston with a turnip and play tennis'

Anne turned to the court with a single brow raised.

'And this is the best reason the wisest men in England could conjure for my incarceration. That I'm so good at sex, I can do it whilst playing tennis?'

Cromwell's eyes wandered over Anne's stays.

'Exactly.'

Anne felt the statement spoke for itself.

'Now we shall begin the questioning.' Cromwell flounced with all the ceremony he could muster. 'Is it, or is it not true that you gave a courtier money?'

Anne looked up briefly from examining her fingernails.

'Yes.'

'Aha! You admit it! You're an adulterous whore!'

'Oh yes, because monetary exchanges must equal sex. Honestly, Mr Cromwell, I'm quite insulted that you don't consider me attractive enough to persuade a man to sleep with me without paying him.' Anne raised an eyebrow.

Cromwell made a concerted effort not to look at Anne's cleavage, which, although she wasn't named after it, was still considerable.

'Yes, exactly,' he stuttered. 'There, she admitted it.'

He shuffled some parchments, foam collecting at the corners of his mouth.

'Ahh! Is it, or is it not true, that you have engaged in sexual activities with your own brother?'

The court went silent. The only guns Cromwell had brought to this trial were big, but this one was practically a cannon.

'My brother couldn't fit any more women into his schedule if he tried.'

'You seem to know a great deal about your brother's mating habits?' Cromwell leered.

'Doesn't everyone? He practically sends out a newsletter.'

Several courtiers nodded and stifled laughs.

'Aha! It's a well-known fact that your brother cannot spell. How would he send a newsletter without an accomplice? An accomplice who knows her way around a quill? An accomplice like you!'

The court gasped.

Anne rolled her eyes.

'And is it not true that you have six fingers on your left hand?'

'No, it's not!' Anne held her pentadactyl hand up to the court.

Mutters rolled across the room.

Cromwell pointed a trembling finger at Anne.

'She's made a finger disappear!'

The court in uproar, the decision was made.

Uncle Norfolk passed the sentence.

'Because thou has offended our sovereign, the King's grace, in committing treason against his person, thou hast deserved death, and thy judgement is this: *that thou shalt be burned here within the Tower of London on the Green, else to have thy head smitten off.*'

Anne folded her arms.

'Thanks, Uncle. If you wouldn't mind dropping a note to Mother about this next time you go visiting?'

Kingston nudged Anne in the ribs.

Henry Percy, Anne's ex-fiancé, stood up and swooned.

'What's he collapsing for? He's not the one about to be incinerated,' Anne hissed. She was dragged to the door where Cromwell stood.

'How…unfortunate,' he said.

*

Anne stared out the window again. Kingston fled upon returning her to her room, sure he would be the King's next target.

'Here she is, your majesty.' Cromwell's voice floated down the corridor.

'Just what I need,' Anne muttered.

'Cast your eye! The woman you once loved and trusted, exposed as an incestuous, treasonous, witchy traitor.'

The King pressed his face against the bars of her cell and dabbed his eyes on the corner of a handkerchief.

'Could I see her? One last time?'

'Of course, your majesty! But be careful not to get too close. Who knows what she may be capable of?' Cromwell unlocked the cell door and the King limped in. He grasped Anne's extremely normal and unmemorable hand.

'My beloved wife, what have you done?'

'I didn't do anything or anyone, Henry, as you well know. How's Jane? I advise her to sign a prenup.'

Henry ignored her.

'Anne, you may be aging, your breasts may be sagging, and you may have produced me a useless, useless daughter, but I'll always cherish the good memories we had together. I'll grant you mercy.'

Anne raised an unhopeful eyebrow at her husband.

'I'll hire the finest French swordsman to chop off your head.'

Silence.

Cromwell nudged her.

'Well, what do you say?'

Anne sighed and unfolded her arms.

'Thanks a lot,' she said, 'I suppose.'

'Farewell, devil's-harlot,' the King said, dabbing his eyes as he hurried out the door to pick table pieces with his next wife.

Cromwell stood behind Anne, but not too close, for she was simultaneously the cheese and the mousetrap.

'If only you had played this differently,' he lamented. 'You could be happily married to me now, raising our deviously intelligent children.'

Anne smiled over her shoulder.

'I'll take the beheading.'

Cromwell's face distorted.

'Good, because that's just what you're going to get,' he sneered, crossing the room in several furious paces.

'Cromwell?' Anne called.

He turned in the doorway, but her gaze remained fixed out of the window. The dying sunlight silhouetted her in a fearsome glow.

'I would just like to remind you, what goes around comes around.'

Famously Dead—
Bite Your Thumb

'We've really shat this up, haven't we?' Juliet said, her blue lips compressed into a thin line.

Romeo stared at his shoes.

'This is conclusive proof that you never listen to me. If the sentence doesn't include the words "Knickers" or "Breasts" you don't care!'

'Ay?' Romeo looked between Juliet's knickers and her breasts hopefully. He thought that sort of thing would be off the table, but when in Verona. Juliet sighed.

'I told you the plan on our wedding night, didn't I? I know your mental faculties may not have had dibs on the blood supply, but I refuse to believe you were rendered brain-dead for the proceeding hour.'

Romeo picked at the label of the empty vial of poison, which still hung about his neck. At least he had the decency to blush.

'I wrote it in your daily planner. Do you remember that? I said "Romeo, I don't think you're listening" and I wrote it down for you? "Tuesday 12th, Juliet fakes her death. Wear black, look sad, don't tell anyone she isn't dead". Did you read that this morning?'

Romeo gave a slight nod.

'What was that?'

'Yes,' he said in a small voice.

'So, what happened?'

'I forgot.'

'I knew you would! I told that useless friar to remind you on the day.'

Romeo sniffed mournfully.

'I didn't get a reminder.'

'I know,' Juliet sighed. 'If I have the capacity to haunt people, he's first on my list.'

'Yeah!' Romeo enthused, eager to share the blame.

Juliet glared at him.

'You forgot,' she muttered. 'How could you possibly forget?'

'Everyone looked so sad, and they kept saying, "Sorry to hear Juliet is dead" and "What a pity about Juliet". After a while, I got a bit…confused.' Romeo gazed at her earnestly.

Juliet, unsure how to respond to idiocy on such a monumental scale, remained silent.

'Still, it was romantic that you killed yourself to be with me,' Romeo said, his mind still hovering around breasts and knickers.

'I didn't kill myself to be with you. I killed myself before your family could do it! Can you imagine if I had walked out of that tomb in one piece? I would have found myself at the bottom of a river in a pair of cement shoes! Besides, I hadn't realised you'd killed Paris. I didn't fancy marrying that old perv.' Juliet flung her arms around, the dagger in her chest wobbling as she spoke. She liked to think Romeo was watching the dagger. She sighed, aware that arguing wouldn't do either of them any good and sat next to Romeo on the coffin lid.

'I suppose I should say it was romantic that you killed yourself to be with me?' Juliet offered.

'It was an accident. I got the bottles mixed up,' Romeo said, still staring at the empty bottle as though learning the difference between cider and cyanide would be valuable to him in death. Juliet rolled her eyes and rescinded the hand she had placed upon his. They sat together, silent and dead. Finally, she said:

'This whole thing is so embarrassing.'

The good friar entered the tomb, shouted, 'Oh, shit!,' lifted his robes and disappeared back through the door.

Juliet watched him, increasingly passive, as death settled upon her.

'I hope this blows over soon and nobody mentions this mortifying debacle ever again.'

Famously Bitten—
Pain in the Asp

Three of Octavian's men rushed into the tomb, steel clattering, loincloths swinging.

'Bollocks,' Syphilus said, upon witnessing the carnage.

Gaseous nudged the nearest body with his toe.

'What do you reckon happened, boss?'

Syphilus put his hands on his hips and rocked on his heels.

'Poisonin',' he said with certainty. A short but educational stint in the Roman army taught him that if you were going to say anything, it was better said with certainty.

'Poisonin'?' Bigamus grunted. 'Like drunked poison?'

'Nah, probably got one of them poisonous snakes to bite her,' Gaseous answered for Syphilus. Bigamus, who had never advanced off his training tablet, knitted his brows together in concentration.

'I don't see no snake, boss,' he finally said.

'Probably hidin' somewhere,' Syphilus shrugged.

Gaseous and Bigamus lifted their sandals cautiously, in case it was 'hidin'' beneath a shoe.

'I still can't see it.' Bigamus scratched his helmet.

'Of course not, Milite,' Syphilus snapped. 'Otherwise it wouldn't be hidin', it would be…exhibitioning.'

'I don't reckon she used a live snake, boss,' Gaseous interjected. 'How did she get it here? Deadly snakes don't take kind to travelin'. I reckon she got one of them people-who-does-the-afterlife to turn its poison into a balm, what she rubbed on her skin.'

Gaseous nurtured a vivid imagination in the same way a fly might nurture a Venus flytrap. Syphilus, who prided himself on possessing as little imagination as it was possible to possess without lacking the creativity to convert oxygen into CO^2, stared at him blankly. During these dangerous seconds, Bigamus developed an opinion:

'I don't reckon so. For the venom to be effective, it must have entered her bloodstream. I reckon she done it intravenously like. You know, with a needle.'

Syphilus stared at him, intellectual theories such as these don't tend to manifest themselves in the minds of people who spent most of their educational years trying to discover whether it was possible to write rude words with an abacus, (it was, a little of Gaseous' imagination was all that was required).

'No, no, no,' Gaseous replied. 'A balm would work if she scratched herself first. Then it would enter her bloodstream. No trouble.'

'Don't be ridiculous. The cut would have to be significantly deep, or the blood would coagulate. Do you see a cut? Forget about the needle, what about a vapour....' Bigamus continued.

Cleopatra's ghost sat on a rock with her fingers stuffed into her ears.

'Does it bloody matter?' she grumbled to Anubis, who shrugged. Death had done nothing to improve her temperament.

Famously Maiden—
Marry Men

'You're completely pooh-poohing the idea.'

Marian kneaded her temples, ignoring the muttering of her colleagues.

'I'm not pooh-poohing it; I'm just saying I don't think you've properly thought through the socio-economic impacts of forced wealth redistribution!'

Robin brandished his Arrow of Emphasis at her, (the Arrow of Emphasis was used for gesturing and underlining particularly important parts of the lessons, the serrated tip offering an additional incentive to avoid caning).

'This is why we don't have women on the team! You're making everything complicated; it's a simple matter of rich vs poor—social ectopics have nothing to do with it!'

'Pah! It has everything to do with it! What do you think will happen when rich people lose money, eh? They'll increase taxes on the poor, and when the money you've given them runs out, they'll be worse off than before!'

'Nu-uh! Then we will just steal the money back again and re-give it to the poor!'

'Who will give it back to the rich in taxes!'

'What do you suggest then, if you're so clever?' Robin shouted, waving his arrow with increasing menace.

'I *told* you, we use the stolen money to buy up land, then give the *land* to poor families. They then grow and sell crops without owing any to the feudal state. This gives peasants the chance to make significant profit and in efficient tools and additional labour. Then you put your men to good use by offering them the military protection previously provided by the lord, in exchange for a very small fee. Your men now have full-time jobs as peacekeepers. The peasants employ more

39

labourers who they grant similar opportunities, the practice becomes widespread, the entire feudal system fails, we enter an entirely private, labour-owned, free-market economy. Now, the problem with free-market economy—'

'Wait, you're suggesting we put the poor in charge?'

'Well, in a manner of speaking, in charge of the economy…'

'What good would that do them, eh? They're *poor*. What they need is money, which is where the plan comes in—'

'But the plan doesn't provide a long-term solution!' Marian said, fighting the urge to raise her voice.

Robin raised his brows at the other Merry Men, who raised their brows back sympathetically.

'That's enough, thank you, Marian. I can see you've given this a lot of thought, but before you strain yourself, you should stop thinking. You're very good at holding babies and distributing bread, but you should leave thinking to people who understand, okay? Let's go through the plan one more time. Marian. It's very simple. Try to keep up?'

Marian took a deep breath and gestured for Robin to continue.

'Step one: Steal from the Rich. Has everyone got that?'

The Merry Men nodded, writing this diligently on their bits of stolen parchment.

Robin gave them several minutes to become comfortable with this information.

'Alright, are we all ready? Little John, what is it? If it's a spelling question, ask the friar.'

Little John's hand scratched his ear on its way back down to his side.

'Anyone else? Will? No, that's fine, pictures are encouraged. I like the detail. You can really see the menace in the rich man's eyes. Let's move on. Step Two:'

Robin sighed.

'What, Marian?'

'You don't feel the need to…elaborate at all?'

Robin used the Arrow of Emphasis to point at the carved tree bark bearing the entire eight-word plan.

'Steal from the rich; if the rich have something, take it. If you see a rich person, and they have a thing, whatever it might be, remove it from their possession. I can't simplify it anymore!'

'This is why we don't let women in the church,' the good friar muttered. 'They have this much trouble with two instructions. Imagine what would happen if they were required to remember ten!'

The Merry Men around him nodded, casting irritated looks at Marian who was, yet again, making them late for lunch.

'Alright, let's put socio-economics to one side for a moment.' Marian's voice rose in frustration. 'What constitutes as rich? If you're starving on the street, anyone who isn't starving is rich to you, aren't they? What's the line between rich and poor? Do we help rich people who have become poor? What if we help the poor people so much they become rich? Do we re-steal it and give it back to the rich people—who are now, in fact, poor? What if someone else has already stolen the rich person's money? Do we steal their clothes as well, just because they're rich?'

Robin fixed a sympathetic smile on his face and encouraged the other Merry Men to do the same.

'Marian, you need to calm down. There's no need to be so aggressive. We're all part of the Merry Team, here.'

'I'm not aggressive! I just—'

'Now you're being argumentative! If you want people to like you, Marian, you should talk less and smile more. No, it's alright, but we're moving on. I can't afford to give any more time to your irrelevant musings. Right. Step Two: give to the poor.'

The scribbling intensified, as did the hatred behind Marian's stare. Robin wandered up and down behind the Merry Board Members.

'That's P—O—O—R, Much Miller, the other is what you do with custard…Davy Doncaster, if I see you do that to Mr Greenleaf again, I'll report you to the friar for the sin of perversion, do you understand?'

Marian wrote nothing otherwise Robin may have suffered the first fatal paper-cut. Robin returned to the front tree.

'Right, have we all got that?' There was general nodding and a murmur of agreement.

'As Lady Marian didn't feel the need to make any notes, perhaps she would like to explain the concept to the class?' Robin said, using his body to shield the words on the tree.

Marian rolled her eyes.

'She's trying to look at your notes!' Much hissed to Alan. A. Dale, who scrabbled to cover his parchment.

'I'm not—' she began.

'See boys, a direct consequence of not listening—'

'Steal from the rich and give to the poor!' Marian bellowed.

Several birds threw themselves from their trees, screaming.

Robin did not move, his mouth agape. Marian's cheeks blazed under the scrutiny of every member of the Merry Meeting, then Robin clapped, very, very slowly.

His clapping became more enthused, and he encouraged the other members of the Merry Team to join him. Soon there was a great deal of whooping and yelling and shouts of 'Hazzah!'. Marian's dark eyes bored into Robin's head.

'Well done, Marian. You've made some real progress today. We understand that not every member of the Merry Team can be a genius, but everyone should try their best.'

There was a crunching as Marian's teeth were ground into non—existence. Robin moved on.

'Excellent. Well, if no one else has anything—'

Much to everyone's surprise, it was not Marian who raised her hand, (but it was Marian who unsheathed a dagger beneath the table).

'Will Scarlett? Is there something you want to add?'

Will stood up to answer, his knees intent on taking the desk with them.

'Yessir, I was just thinking, sir, what do we do with the loot *between* taking it from the rich and giving it to the poor?'

Robin sat down on the head tree stump and scratched his head with the tip of the arrow.

'I hadn't thought of that.'

Marian, seeing they would not be excused for lunch until the query was settled, raised a hand.

Robin ignored it.

She spoke anyway.

'Why don't we collect the wealth in a mutually agreeable spot, and hold a monthly meeting to decide how to distribute it?'

There was silence. A few of the Merry Men scratched their ears. Robin kneaded his forehead.

'Marian, you were doing so well! That would never work! One meeting per month? Do I look like I'm made of time?' he shook his head. 'You've done enough thinking for one day!'

He seized the parchment in front of Marian, (which had nothing on it but an excellent artist's interpretation of Robin's head exploding) and placed it in the waste-parchment basket.

'Does anyone have a *decent* suggestion?'

After a while, Arthur Bland raised an arm.

'I was just thinking…'

'Go on?' Robin nodded encouragingly.

'Well, why don't we find some place we all agree on to store the loot, and once every, pfft, I don't know, two months or so? We could meet up and decide who should get what.'

Robin walked around the backs of the seated men, arrow in hand. A few of them twitched as he passed behind them, rubbing the ghosts of wounds from previous meetings.

Robin thrust a hand into Arthur Bland's hair and ruffled it up.

'An excellent idea! Ah, I'm so proud of you! I knew you wouldn't live up to your name all your life!'

'Oi, that was my idea!' Marian said, getting to her feet.

Robin wagged a finger.

'It doesn't matter who thought up what first. We're all part of the Merry Team. Besides, his idea is completely different, vastly improved. No silly suggestions about monthly meetings!'

'If her mood tonight is any indication of what time of the month it is, I'm not signing myself up for that!' the friar muttered, elbowing Gilbert Whitehand, who, usually the butt of the joke himself, tittered mercilessly.

'Get stuffed, Friar Tuck!' Marian leapt at him. Several of the braver (or more stupid) members of Team Merry leapt in front of the good friar, but most of them had evolved a better sense of self-preservation.

Robin slammed the Arrow of Emphasis on the tree and called for silence as the Merry Men attempted to separate the pair.

Prior to this event, Friar Tuck, like every other friar in England, had a beautiful and thorough head of hair. After this event, the friar was forced to sport a hairstyle so stupid that the other monks considered it an advanced form of self-flagellation and adopted it themselves. The sizeable chunk of hair removed from the centre was gripped tightly in Marian's hand as she was escorted back to her seat.

When peace once again reigned, Robin squatted down and placed an arm around Marian's shoulder, shielding them from the prying ears of the rest of the men.

'Marian. Look at me, please. Do you think that was appropriate, what you did to the Friar? Ah! I don't want to know who started it; do you think it was appropriate? No, I didn't think so.'

Marian folded her arms, her hairy prize still triumphantly in her grasp.

'The boys let you in here today—despite your blatant disregard for the office dress code—' (he gestured to the breeches she had donned. She seethed. Did he know how much fabric went into a skirt? Where was she supposed to find that in the middle of the forest?) '—and all you have done so far is disrupt this meeting.'

Marian made to interrupt. Robin raised a benevolent hand.

'Is there something you want to say to the Merry Team?'

Marian shook her head.

'Look at them, Marian. Robin Hood and his Miserable Men doesn't have the same ring to it. Is there something you want to say?'

A twig snapped somewhere in the near vicinity. Robin wheeled around. There was silence filled only with the oppressive stares of dozens of unseen eyes. Suddenly, a whinny and a cry cracked through the trees. Dozens of hoofbeats caused the stones on the forest floor to leap and dance.

'It's Gisborne and his men! They've found us! To arms!' Robin bellowed. The Merry Men scrabbled from their seats, their parchment flying as weapons were produced from a creative array of orifices.

As the battle ensued, the dark and educated Guy of Gisborne appeared through the trees, mounted on his night-black steed, his black uniform shining in the evening rays. His eyes flicked calmly over the chaos. He was searching for something—someone. Robin's men were losing, although they were putting up a good fight considering the crudeness of their weapons; the Arrow of Emphasis currently emphasising the missing eye of the closest guard. Eventually, Guy found her, a dark smirk forming about his thin lips. He urged his horse to trot delicately across the clearing, trampling several Merry Men beneath its enormous hooves. Upon reaching her, he held out a muscular arm.

Marian realised she did, indeed, have something to say:

'I always have had a weakness for a man in leather,' she sighed.

Governments are always much easier to topple from within, after all.

Famously Fiery—
How Do You Solve a Problem like Boudicca?

'Order, order!' Claudius said, banging his hand hard on the table in an act of officious self-sacrifice.

As per usual, the other councillors ignored him. It always was a mistake to have lunch meetings with Roman councillors. Trying to keep everyone sat down long enough to commence was difficult when someone was always popping off for a quick vomit or something even more unhygienic. Then, just as everyone settled, the next course came in, causing even more uproar as everyone fought for their slice of eyeball. Claudius spied the primae mensae making its way down the corridor and gestured for the slaves to make themselves scarce before the other men saw it.

He stood and slammed his cup down until it threatened to buckle, and the ivory trim of the table threatened to crack.

'Are you bloody listening? I'm calling this meeting to *order*!'

This was a special tone of voice Claudius usually reserved for assassination attempts and brought instant quiet over the group of men.

'As I'm sure we're all aware, I've called this meeting because we have to decide what exactly to put in our letter to Imperator Nero— may the Gods bless his beloved and virile instrument.'

'Well, that's easy? We'll tell him some woman rallied thousands of Britons, captured several major cities, killed most of the civilians therein, gave our best general an almighty whoopin' and exposed several points of weakness in our rule so the next rebellion is likely to be more successful unless we swiftly alter our approach to governance,' Ludacrus said, cheerfully.

The room was silent, aside from the gentle hiss of the under-floor heating.

'Alright, we're not going to tell him that,' Claudius said at last.

'Then…what are we going to tell him, boss?' Normus asked from the far end of the table. He was eager to return to his gustatio—the asparagus was getting cold.

'The truth, obviously.' Claudius spread his hands, the arms of his toga floating out like the wings of a benevolent angel.

'But what Ludacrus said—'

'—was one way of remembering the events. That isn't how I remember them at all.'

Normus, by speaking first, had apparently nominated himself as spokesperson.

'How do you remember it, boss?' he asked in a small voice.

'Good of you to ask, Normus. Hmm…I remember the woman in question was oh, probably half giant? Long matted hair, piercing eyes, a voice that could circumcise men…' Claudius raised his eyebrows meaningfully.

'Nah, boss, you were drinking too much wine. She was a little scrap of a thing—'

'No, Normus. It is you who are misremembering. She was obviously gigantic, and probably a witch or demon. Wouldn't you say, Suetonius?'

Suetonius had hoped to get through the meeting without saying anything at all. It was he who was supposed to be a great general, and he who had lost to a girl. Three times.

'I—yes, I suppose…' he managed.

'Very good. See Normus? Suetonius remembers. Now why did she attack? I recall, it was outrageous…' Claudius continued.

'Ah…'

'Quite right, Normus, the previous King of the Iceni tried to put a woman on the throne. One of his daughters, yes. No! Wait, make it two. Two daughters he named as heirs in direct defiance of the Romanic system. Excellent…and I mustn't forget to mention all the violence the Iceni were subjected to when we sorted them out…and that rape...mustn't forget that, sex sells after all, heh, heh...'

The men around the table exchanged glances. Not only was Claudius holding a conversation with himself, almost all of what he was saying was just...wrong?

'Boss, I don't mean to be rude, but some of that is definitely not true, the woman for a start—'

'What experience do you have with women, eh, Normus?' Claudius said, slamming his hand onto the table. Normus didn't make eye contact with the slave girl pouring wine, but she giggled nonetheless. Claudius ignored this.

'Can we finish this letter, please? The sooner it's finished, the sooner we can...return to our duties. Where were we? Ah yes, we had slaughtered the Iceni nobles...' Claudius' stylus flew across his tablet. Occasionally he stopped to rub out an indentation in the wax with a warm finger, then chuckled and carried on.

'There we are. Now...where did she attack first? Oh! The old people's home in Camulodunum...'

Normus said nothing, so Dorkius raised a tentative hand.

'No sir, she started—'

'Shh!'

Dorkius lowered his hand and Claudius sighed, finishing his sentence and placing his stylus on the table.

'Dorkius, think for a moment. What would you have liked to have happened?'

'Sir?'

'In an ideal world, hypothetically speaking and all that?'

'Hypothetically speaking? I suppose I would have...liked us to have triumphantly defeated her forces?'

'It's a good thing that's what happened, then.'

'What?'

'I think what Claudius is saying,' Normus said slowly, 'Is that it doesn't matter if we recall things a little...differently to the mighty

48

Imperator, because he's probably not going to come over here to check.'

'Exactly, Normus! Plus, only we have a reliable written database—the Britons can say whatever they want around the fire, but who will remember that in fifty years' time? What I'm *saying* is it's not our fault if some details get......misremembered.'

There was the gentle coo as the rest of the table caught up.

'Finally, I think we are starting to remember the same thing! Let's try this again. How many rebels were there?'

'Ten thousand?'

'Think bigger, Dorkius!'

'One hundred thousand!'

'That's right!'

'Three hundred thousand!'

'Alright, Dorkius, that's almost a tenth of the population of Britain. We'll go with something around the two-hundred and fifty thousand mark…' Claudius made a note.

'How many of us were there?'

'When?' Suetonius piped up.

'In the final battle, of course, where she was humiliatingly defeated!'

'Ah, at least five-hundred thousand…' Suetonius said, scratching his head. He wasn't used to doing sums without an abacus and the fingers and toes of at least three slaves.

'*No*, Suetonius, do you not remember? At least four-hundred thousand were incapacitated…' Claudius pressed, determined they would all have the hang of it by the time class was dismissed.

'What? No—'

'And, if you recall, of the remaining one hundred thousand, ninety thousand had caught one of those ghastly English colds…'

'Right…' Suetonius said, straining to remember. 'So that leaves…'

'Ten thousand, exactly,'

'Ten thousand men? Against two-hundred and fifty thousand

savage, bloodthirsty tribesmen? Did we win?'

Claudius kneaded his temples.

'Yes, Suetonius, you did win—you were there, remember?'

'Yes, but I recall—'

'You recall wrong!' Claudius said, shrilly.

Dorkius elbowed Suetonius hard in the side.

'Ah, right…so maybe they didn't just kill people, they tortured them as well? I just forgot?' Suetonius suggested.

'Exactly! Think of the noble women they impaled on spikes!' Claudius winked.

'Yeah! They had their boobs cut off and sewn onto their mouths!' So many of the heads round the table turned to face Ludacrus that the room resembled a coin collection.

'Why would anyone want to sew anyone's boobs to their mouths? I mean, aside from being time-consuming and unnecessary, it's a logistical nightmare. Boobs come in all different sizes. What do you do if they're an extreme of size? How are you going about applying them, one boob over the entire mouth? A cleavage beneath the nose? What about—'

'Thank you, Drearius,' Dorkius interrupted, holding a napkin to his mouth. 'Let's not go into details. Just make it grim, make it gory, make it…barbaric!'

'We could put that she played the fiddle while she did it!' Ludacrus enthused.

'The only way I would let that make it into this letter would be if Rome was burning!' Dorkius snapped, 'The lyre is a much more dignified and invented instrument.'

'Finally, we've all got the hang of it!' Claudius said cheerfully, his hand flying to keep up with the ideas. 'I'll pop the bit about the boobs in somewhere near the end…'

Other interesting words flew around the table, such as 'cannibal', 'nymphomaniac' and 'Red-head', but Claudius wasn't stupid. He knew when things were threatening to go too far. The trick to getting away with a lie lay mostly within its believability.

Triumphantly, he formed the final letter.

'Excellent! This is perfect. I shall have a slave copy it and send it to Nero with the morning post. Good job, men. Let us celebrate this mighty and auspicious victory with double the food and double the wine!'

The table cheered and clattered the crockery, relieved to be released from duty without having to stab anyone in the back.

Suetonius nudged Claudius in the ribs.

'That was quite brilliant, you know. I might use that myself in our next battle...'

Claudius drained his cup and offered it to a slave to refill.

'Ha, certainly, use away! That's the great thing about right now— there's only ever a few blokes writing anything down, they're usually doing it at least a few decades later, and they're almost always on our side! To be quite honest, we could spin most of history however we damn well please!'

Famously Female—
Bonny Wee Lass

Shadows flickered in the candlelight against the walls of the hold. Wispy, ghost-like shadows with reaching fingers projected against the weathered wood. One gust of wind through the cracks of the aging ship and, with a hiss, they would be plunged into darkness.

Jim, the cabin boy, shuffled up his hammock until he was as close as he dared to be to the ship's cat. Mr Sauvage was not, in truth, a cat. He was several lumps of cat fur clinging desperately to a skeleton which, if one squinted, bore a vague resemblance to that of a cat. He was also fiercely bad-tempered. If Jim sought comfort, he was probably better off asking Mr Brine, the gnarled master gunner, who once utilised his own mother's false teeth as ammunition—while she was still attached to them, then turning to Mr Sauvage.

'Do ye hear that?' Eddie 'Rambling' Thackeray, the Boatswain, jumped, causing a Mexican wave of jumps to shiver down the bunk room. In his spare time, Thackeray liked to apply himself to 'readin'. The issue was, he was entirely unable to distinguish fact from fiction. If it was in a book, he reasoned that nobody would have bothered to write it unless what it said was true. Last week, Thackeray had finished a book about superstitions at sea, and since then, one couldn't break wind without Thackeray attempting to read the odour like tea leaves.

'Jeysus, Thackeray,' No-Knob Norman muttered, 'if you're going to jump at every creek and fart on this ship it's going to be a long bloody night.'

'I told you. We're listening for a woman.'

'Why doesn't Dry-Bones Jones hide under Mr Brine's hammock again, and we'll listen to him scream like a little girl?'

Mr Brine's glower cut the throat of the laughs on their way out.

'I ain't laughing! All signs suggest there's a woman aboard. The composition of my stew, the three seagulls—'arbingers of death! And

I'm telling you, that mouse squeaked three times!' Thackeray continued, stony-faced.

'So? What does that prove?'

'Because, it says so, 'ere, in me book: If a…ship…'as bad luck…or…'arbingers appear…unto…'em…surely there is…a wumun…onboard. Clear as day.'

Thackeray held out the book for Norman to inspect. He confirmed that it was, indeed, a book.

'Where is she then, this woman?' Norman pressed.

Thackeray slammed his book indignantly.

' 'ow am I supposed to know? I'm trained in readin' the signs. I ain't got hoccult knowledge!'

'Right. What do we do when we find her? There ain't no port anywhere close. Do we throw 'er overboard?'

'Course not! We take 'er clothes off. It's a well-known fact that a naked woman calms the sea.'

Dry-Bones scratched beneath his eye patch. 'Well known, you say?'

Suddenly, Thackeray and Jim were alone in the bunk room.

Some sexists amongst you may assume that the men were eager to find a woman, as six months at sea had left them sex-starved. Incorrect. They all needed a haircut, some socks darned and a short emotional therapy session—they hoped for a dumpling-bosomed mother figure rather than a trim vestal virgin.

'How will we know if they've found her, Mr Thackeray?' Jim asked.

'We'll know, lad. She'll scream, for sure.'

'Do women always scream then?'

'They do if No-Knob introduces himself with his party trick.'

'Oh,' Jim pondered. 'I don't know much about women.'

'There ain't much to know. They're like cats, put a bit of food down now and then and they mostly take care of themselves,' Thackeray said, which is a great many words to illustrate that Thackeray didn't know much about women either.

The door to the bunk room flew open, and a disgruntled crew filed back in.

'Not a bird in sight. Not even 'er bloomers,' Norman said.

'That ain't strictly true,' Dry-Bones said, returning to his seat. 'Brine found a pair of Bloomers. I saw 'im, he sniffed them, then put 'em in his pocket.'

'I did not!'

'You did too! You dirty bloomer-sniffer!' Dry-Bones squared up to him.

'Stop it!' Thackeray muscled between them. 'Now, Mr Brine, if you 'ave, by any chance, come across a pair of bloomers, it would be in your best in'erest to share them. It says 'ere in me book that anyone carryin' somethin' of a woman will be smote the worst.'

'It don't say that!' Mr Brine challenged.

'It does, 'ere!' Thackeray stuck the book under his nose, knowing full well that Brine couldn't read.

'Oh aye,' Brine mumbled, thrusting the bloomers into Thackeray's hand and returning to his seat.

'Told ya,' Dry-Bones muttered. Brine glowered at him.

'I was only keepin' 'em safe, so the woman couldn't put 'em back on!' he protested.

'Good thinking!' Thackeray said, pocketing the bloomers himself. 'I'll keep them for further testing.'

No one protested, no one wished to be smote by the harbingers of doom, or enlightened as to the particular protocols involved in further testing.

'What now?' Norman said. 'There's a bird on the boat, but we can't find 'er! She ain't out there, I 'ad to stop One-Word from ripping up the floorboards. We 'ad a long, 'ard look.'

'I'm sure you did,' Thackeray said, his mind on the bloomers in his pocket. Jim nudged him.

'Quite right, No-Knob. Well, if she ain't out there, it stands to reason she must be…in 'ere!'

The men looked around the empty bunk room. The only furniture was one table and twelve hammocks. Although there is a lot to be said for the humble hammock, they don't make particularly good hiding places for anything larger than a hamster.

'In 'ere?' Dry-Bones echoed.

'Yes! I'm sayin' she could be one of us!'

'One of us could be a bird?'

'Yes! It 'appens all the time, women reckonin' they can impersonate men an' sneak aboard a ship to reunite with a long-lost love. 'appened twice in the book I finished last month. We'll weed 'er out…There's an easy way to settle this, lads. Trousers down! Jim-Lad, grab some parchment and we'll make notes as we go.'

'You what?'

'Trousers down, Dry-Bones, we've all got to be checked.'

'What are we checking for?'

'What do you think we're checking for, man, skidmarks? We're makin' sure that there's the traditional assortment. One of one and two of the other.'

No-Knob Norman stood awfully, uncomfortably close to Rambling Thackeray. A revolver had appeared from the depths of his trousers (weapon concealment was one of the few advantages of his unfortunate condition).

'An' what happens, pray tell, if someone is a couple of the other short?'

Thackeray inspected a dust mite in the far corner.

'Maybe I've made a mistake,' he finally said.

'Aye?'

'We're not looking for a *lack* of something, but an *abundance* of something else.'

Norman clapped Thackeray on the shoulder.

'That's alright then, because what I've got left, I've definitely got in abundance...' he winked at Jim, who was still holding the blank parchment in a confused daze.

'Not *that*, I'm sayin' that ladies can do lady things. They can cook—
'

Cook sharpened his carving knife.

'I mean, sew—'

The sailmaker unsheathed a needle.

'I mean, clean! Oh, it's no use.' Thackeray reversed onto a barrel, head in hands.

' 'ow can it be this 'ard! Women should smell nice, have nice hair, 'n wear dresses. They shouldn't be piratin' in the first place. It's like there's hardly any difference between man an' woman at all!'

The crew hovered in various states of undress, waiting for Thackeray's next orders. Norman had removed all his clothes and was adamantly telling One-Word Bill that it wasn't the number of beans in the stew that mattered. It was how far you could make it stretch. To everyone's surprise, Bill's reply comprised of two words. Norman shoved Bill. Bill shoved Norman. Norman fell into his hammock. Mr Sauvage attacked Norman. Norman wished he was wearing pants. Norman's new nickname is No-Nothing Norman.

Amongst the commotion, Thackeray sat on his barrel, head in hands, staring dismally at the family of rats which were currently in congregation on top of the copy of the Bible he had leant to Mr Brine. He fancied he could even tell the male from the female rats from here, because of course, the female rats would all have longer fur, an' boobs an' things. Wouldn't they? Jim tugged at Thackeray's sleeve.

'P'haps we should tell the captain?'

'Good thinkin', boy! The Captain will have found stray women before. He'll know what to do! As you've been a good lad, you can come with me.'

Jim was not sure this was an honour he wanted, having made the suggestion to shock Thackeray into forgetting about the whole thing. A man wired like a barrel of Dynamite, the captain's diet consisted exclusively of grog, having sworn off the harder stuff after a disastrous sherry-and-new-ship related incident in his youth. He was not a man to be trifled with. His sobriety made him chronically irritable but also sharper than a sword fish who has got his nose caught in a pencil sharpener. It was like the captain could see through walls, could sense disquiet, could smell disaster, (which, when the ship's cook and the manager of the latrines were one in the same person, was not usually difficult).

Thackeray squared his hat upon his head and lead the way upstairs to the captain's cabin. He rapped on the door with near suicidal confidence.

'What?' the captain barked through the door.

'Tis I, Ca'pn, Rambling Thackeray. I've bad news.'

The door opened and the black eyes of the captain peered out.

'Is it a mutiny? Tell 'em to get back to work. Do they know what happened to my last mutineers? No, neither do I. I couldn't see for the fire nor hear for the screams.'

'You're the embodiment of diplomacy, sir, but taint that.'

'What then, am I speaking to Rambling Thackeray or has One-Word Bill lost six inches vertically and gained them horizontally?'

'I'm afraid it's mighty serious, I reckon, from my deducin', we has a *woman* on board, sir.'

The captain's raised a hand to stroke his enormous beard.

'A woman you say? That's mighty serious indeed. Pretty is she? No matter, send her up to my cabin, Thackeray…'

'No Sir. I reckons we 'ave a woman on board who is disguised as a man.'

'Ah. Well, that's quite different.'

The captain joined them in the corridor. He was a small man, slight with dark eyes and a mass hair of he kept beneath the remnants of a hat. Incredibly, nobody had taken issue with the Captain's size. This was because his smallness made him fast as whipcrack, and it's hard to finish a sentence when the lower half of your jaw is swinging near your bellybutton.

'What evidence do you have of this *woman*?'

'When I stirred my stew last night, three chunks of potato bobbed to the top—that initially aroused my suspicion.'

'I'm not interested in the state of your suspicion, but I assume this came from a book on root-vegetable reading?'

'Yessir, although the potato isn't technically a vegetable—'

'Anything else, Thackeray?'

'Yessir! I went to the john this morning, and it was occupied. I 'ad a look under the door, an' someone was sat down! On the John! Cook ain't made On the Run Puddin' for days now! What would a man who hadn't had a dose of On the Run Puddin' be doin' sat down on the John, sir?'

'That's all, Thackeray?'

'Not all at all, sir, there's the ominous sky, the trio of seagulls, the mice who squeaked three times...and of course, there's these.'

Thackeray pulled the trump card, (or patch of fabric, but that bit was at the back and wasn't pleasant to look at), from his pocket.

The captain raised a hand to halt Thackeray's Ramblings, and, meeting some resistance, took the bloomers from him. He thrust them into his pocket and clicked his heels to attention, urging Thackeray and Jim to imitate.

'Excellent work, Thackeray. I reckon I can see a promotion lingering in your not-too-distant future.'

'Thankyousir, verykindsir,' Thackeray beamed.

'I trust you have done all the normal checks on the crew?'

'Yessir, 'ad a rummage and a strip, but I can't find anything.'

The captain scratched his beard.

'Well, sir,' Thackeray leaned in. 'I don't like to tell tales, but we all know that Norman isn't in possession of the full parcel…'

'Yes, but Mr Knit personally removed the, ah, afflicted part of Mr Norman's appendage. I don't reckon we need to worry about him, do you?'

'Ah, nosir,' Thackeray deflated. Mr Knit would be the one holding the saw if everything went wrong, and he was very easily offended.

The captain continued.

'Done the sniff test?'

'Sniffed every man myself, sir.'

'And the stitch test?'

Thackeray's voice got very small.

'The stitch test?'

'Yes! Surely an heducated man like yourself knows that while men can sew, only a *woman* can sew in a straight line.'

'Really?'

'Are you questioning me, Thackeray?'

'Nosir, notatallsir! I'll get canvas and thread immediately!'

'Excellent. I don't want any material wasted, so p'haps you could perform the test on that no.3 sail that was torn last week?'

Thackeray clicked his heels and retreated backwards down the corridor, dragging Jim with him.

'I'll get to it right away! Come along, Jim, we mustn't bother the ca'pn any longer. Sleep well, sir!'

'You too, Thackeray, and you…boy.' The captain waved them off before returning to his quarters. He shut the door quietly.

'Whowasat?' The dishevelled head of the first mate, beard half falling off, rose from the covers.

'Thackeray. He reckons there's a woman on board.'

The first mate yanked his beard off and sat up.

'Did he suspect anything?'

'No, Mary.' The captain peeled his beard off and placed it on its stand. 'I could sunbathe topless on the poop-deck and he wouldn't

59

notice. He's too busy counting the chunks of potato in his soup. Doesn't mean you shouldn't keep your bloomers to yourself, though,' the captain said, removing them from his pocket and throwing them across the room to his bedfellow.

Mary caught them.

'Bollocks! I hung them out the window to dry. They must have got caught in the wind.'

Mary reached for the captain as he got into bed. 'I'm sorry, Annie. I know I said last time, when I used soap in the bath, that I would be more careful. I do likes being a man, but that doesn't mean I wanna smell like dead seagull.'

'Thackeray was right about one thing. We're having terrible luck on this ship. The wind has been against us since we left port, we've both discovered we're pregnant, old Calico has been unconscious in the war room for three days now…The only way this could get any worse is if we were boarded and arrested!'

Mary snuggled into the crook of the captain's arm, picking stray beard hairs from his chest. Mary shuddered at the thought of the cold, landlocked cell, or worse, the creaking gallows which awaited them if they were caught.

'If we're not bringing the bad luck, what is?'

The captain shrugged. 'Dry-Bones left that ladder propped against the latrine door—fifty men walked under it before Thackeray thought to move it. And we broke that shipment of mirrors. Two thousand mirrors times seven years' bad luck…that's…'

'A lot,' Mary interjected.

The captain nodded.

A cacophony of mewling erupted from a crate beneath the Chart table as Mr Sauvage appeared outside the window, pawing to be let in.

'There's too much superstition around nowadays,' the captain said, placing the cat on top of thirteen jet black balls of fur, mewling indignantly for their dinner.